THE BEAR AND WINTER

THE BEAR AND WINTER

ASHLEY V. TORRES

XULON PRESS

Xulon Press
2301 Lucien Way #415
Maitland, FL 32751
407.339.4217
www.xulonpress.com

Paperback ISBN-13: 978-1-66282-610-8
Ebook ISBN-13: 978-1-66282-611-5

SARAH WAS PLAYING
OUTSIDE, THEN SHE WAS
JUMP ROPING.

SUDDENLY IT GOT COLD
AND WINDY! THE SKY
BECAME GLOOMY.

SARAH WENT IN HER
CAVE. SHE MADE SOME
HOT COCOA.

She watched the storm from her cave. It got really cold.

SARAH WAS SURPRISED.
SHE HAD NEVER SEEN
SNOW BEFORE.

SHE PLAYED AND BUILT
A SNOWMAN.

Acknowledgment

Illustrations by
Ashley V. Torres

CPSIA information can be obtained
at www.ICGtesting.com
Printed in the USA
BVHW022108251021
619844BV00017BA/1278

With Jesus

I AM THANKFUL

Copyrights

www.gnmkids.com

This book belongs to:

_____

Sophie was having fun at the beach.
She built sandcastles, swam in the ocean,
and collected seashells.

Then her mother shouted, "Sophie! It's time to go!"

"Aww," Sophie complained, "I don't want to go!"

Her mother reminded her that they were going to the zoo.
That would be fun!

When they were at the zoo, Sophie began to complain after they had walked around for a bit.

"How much longer, Mama?" she asked.
"I want to go home!"

On the way home in the car, Sophie
complained that she was tired and hungry.

"What's for dinner?" she asked
from the back seat.

"We're having spaghetti,"
her mother replied.

It took forever for the spaghetti to cook!
Sophie grumbled about having to wait for her dinner.

That evening, Sophie's grandad stopped by.

"How was your day, my girl?" he asked.

"Terrible," Sophie answered grumpily.

"Come here," her grandad said,
"I have a story to tell you."

Sophie climbed up on the couch
and sat next to him.

"One day," he began by saying, "ten people who were really sick were healed by Jesus.

But only one person came back to thank him."

Sophie thought about that for a moment. Why did only one person come back to thank Jesus? Weren't they happy that he had made them better?

Then, Sophie's grandad asked her again, "How was your day? Can you think of anything you enjoyed today?"

Instantly, Sophie's eyes lit up. "Oh, yes!
I enjoyed lots of things, Grandad! I enjoyed
collecting seashells at the beach.
I laughed at the silly monkeys at the zoo.
And I enjoyed every bite of Mama's spaghetti.
I was so hungry!"

Sophie's grandad chuckled. Then, he pulled her into a big hug. "See how much better it is to be thankful?"

Sophie nodded and said, "I guess I was paying attention to what I didn't like, instead of thinking about all the good things. I now see how thinking about the good things makes me happy!"

Her grandad nodded and smiled.
"Let's be grateful and thank Jesus.
Because of him, we're able to experience
the beautiful and fun things in life."

"I have one more thing to thank Jesus for."
Sophie said.

"What's that?" Grandpa asked.

"You!"she exclaimed, then gave him a big hug.

As Sophie was about to go to bed, she closed her eyes and bowed her head. Then she said, "Thank you, Jesus, for this wonderful day!"

The End.

In everything give thanks: for this is the will of God in Christ Jesus concerning you.

(1 Thessalonians 5:18 KJV)

Author's note:

Thank you so much for reading this book. If you enjoyed this book, we would love it if you could leave a review and recommend it to a friend.

If there is anything you would like to share with us to help us improve this book, please go to gnmkids.com/feedback

Please checkout our other books

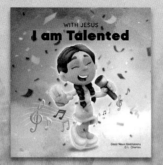

www.gnmkids.com

Made in the USA
Las Vegas, NV
31 October 2024

10466285R00021